Out of the Nursery, Into the Night

Out of the Nursery, Into the Night

By Kathleen Hague · Illustrated by Michael Hague

Methuen Children's Books
London

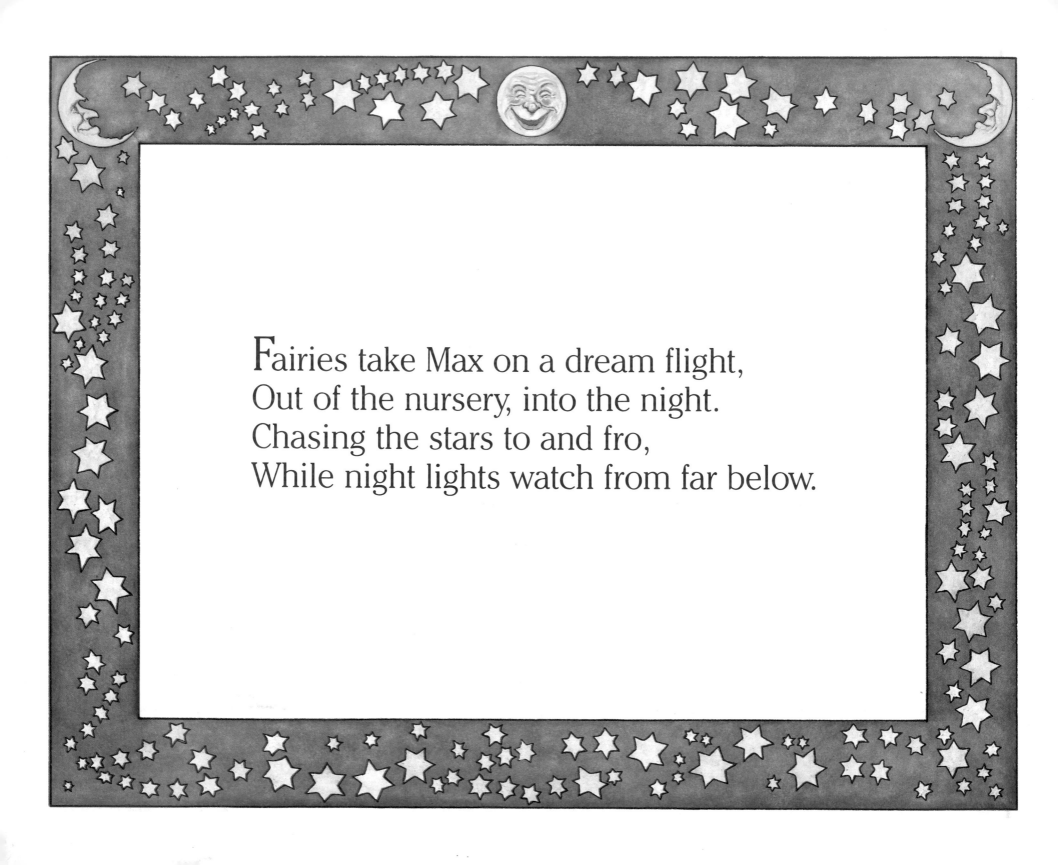

Fairies take Max on a dream flight,
Out of the nursery, into the night.
Chasing the stars to and fro,
While night lights watch from far below.

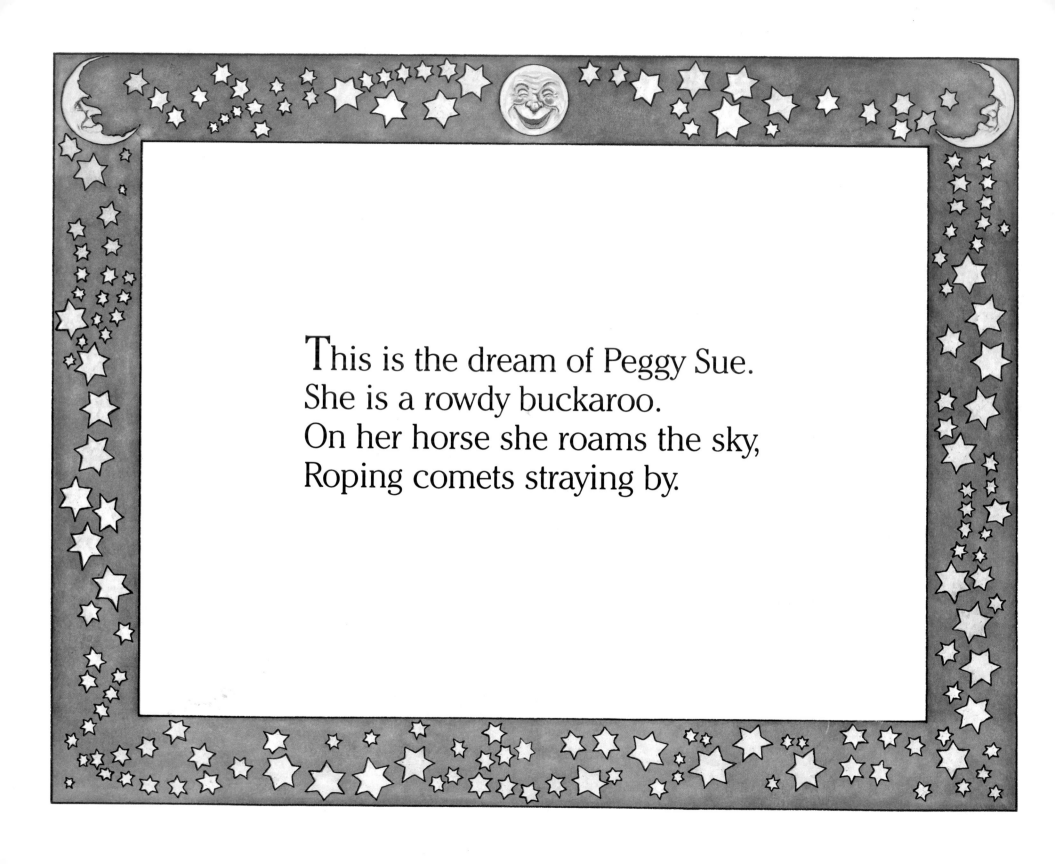

This is the dream of Peggy Sue.
She is a rowdy buckaroo.
On her horse she roams the sky,
Roping comets straying by.

Chris is a knight known far and wide.
Across dream kingdoms he will ride.
Righting wrongs that have been done,
And taming dragons—every one.

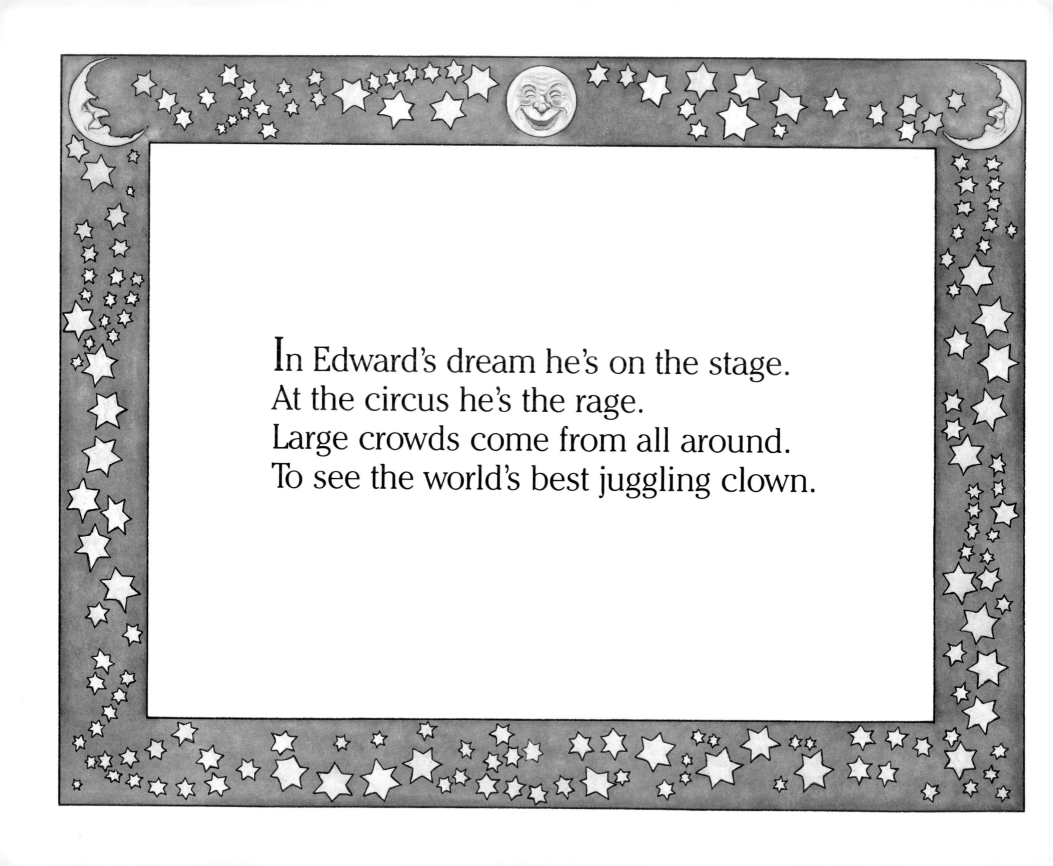

In Edward's dream he's on the stage.
At the circus he's the rage.
Large crowds come from all around.
To see the world's best juggling clown.

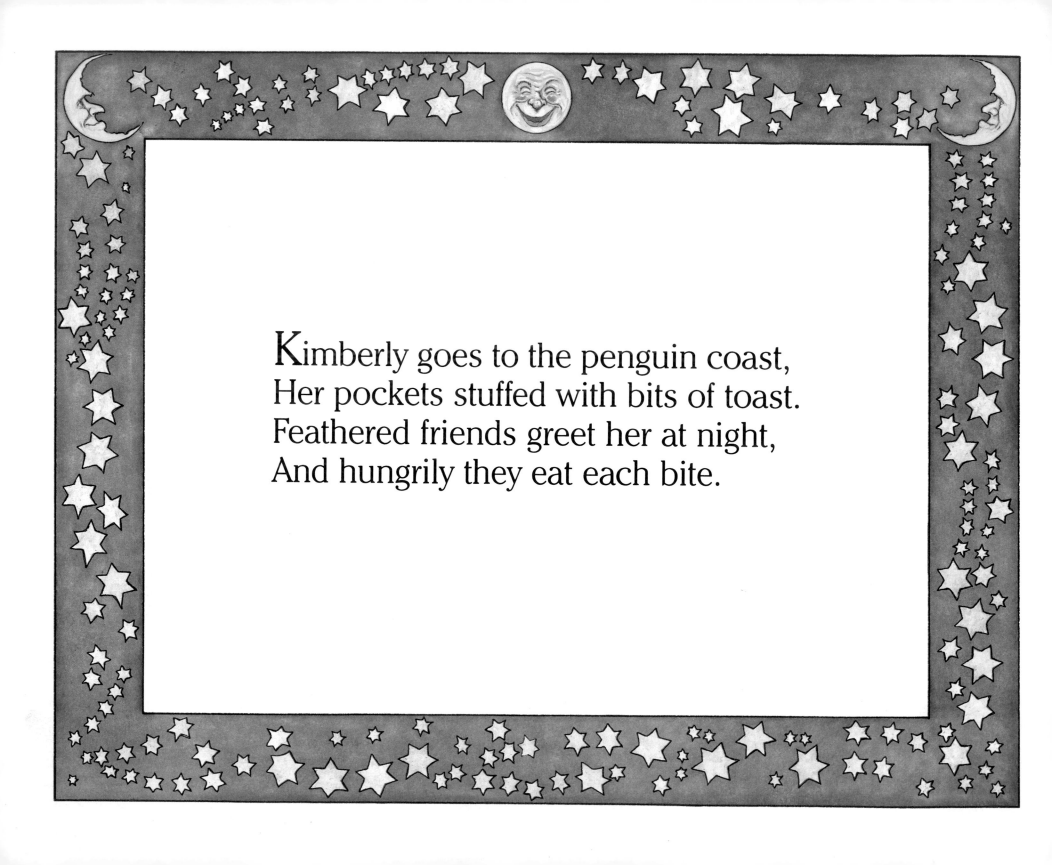

Kimberly goes to the penguin coast,
Her pockets stuffed with bits of toast.
Feathered friends greet her at night,
And hungrily they eat each bite.

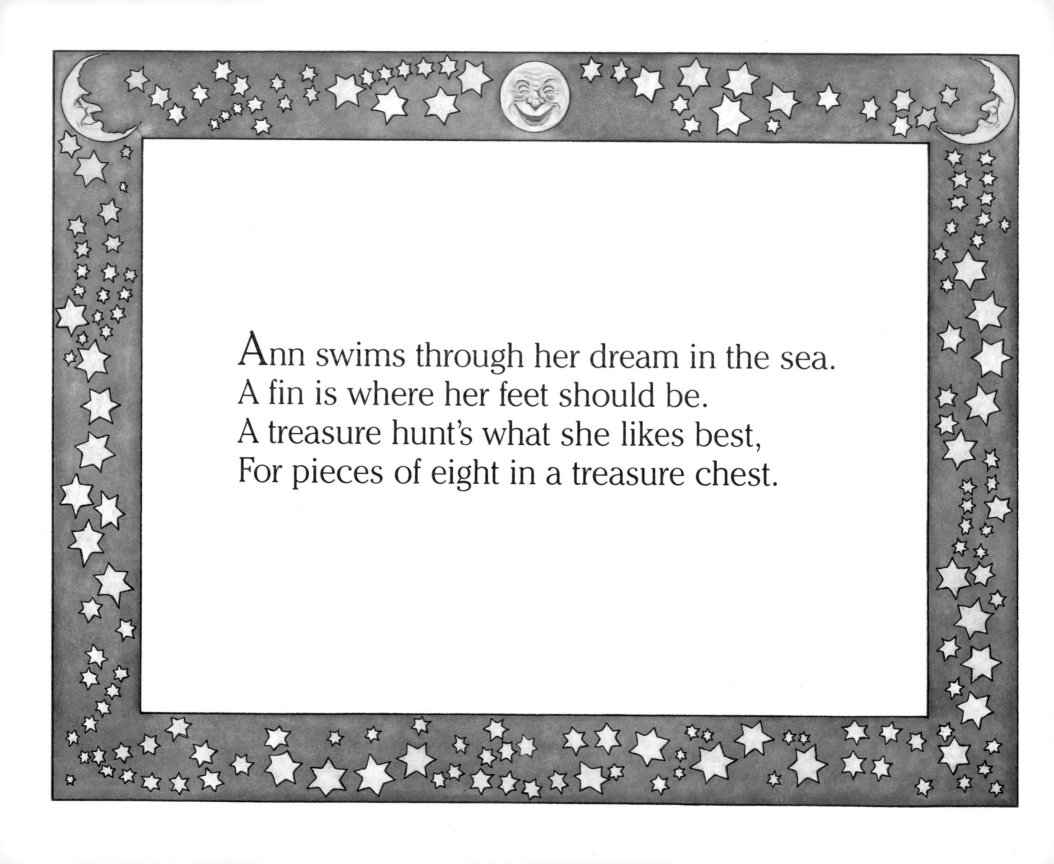

Ann swims through her dream in the sea.
A fin is where her feet should be.
A treasure hunt's what she likes best,
For pieces of eight in a treasure chest.

Bess sees a monster in her dreams.
It's not as scary as it seems.
She made him up in her head,
And now he stands guard by her bed.

Ruth explores an enchanted place,
A look of wonder on her face.
A children's moon hangs in the sky
And listens to Pan's lullaby.

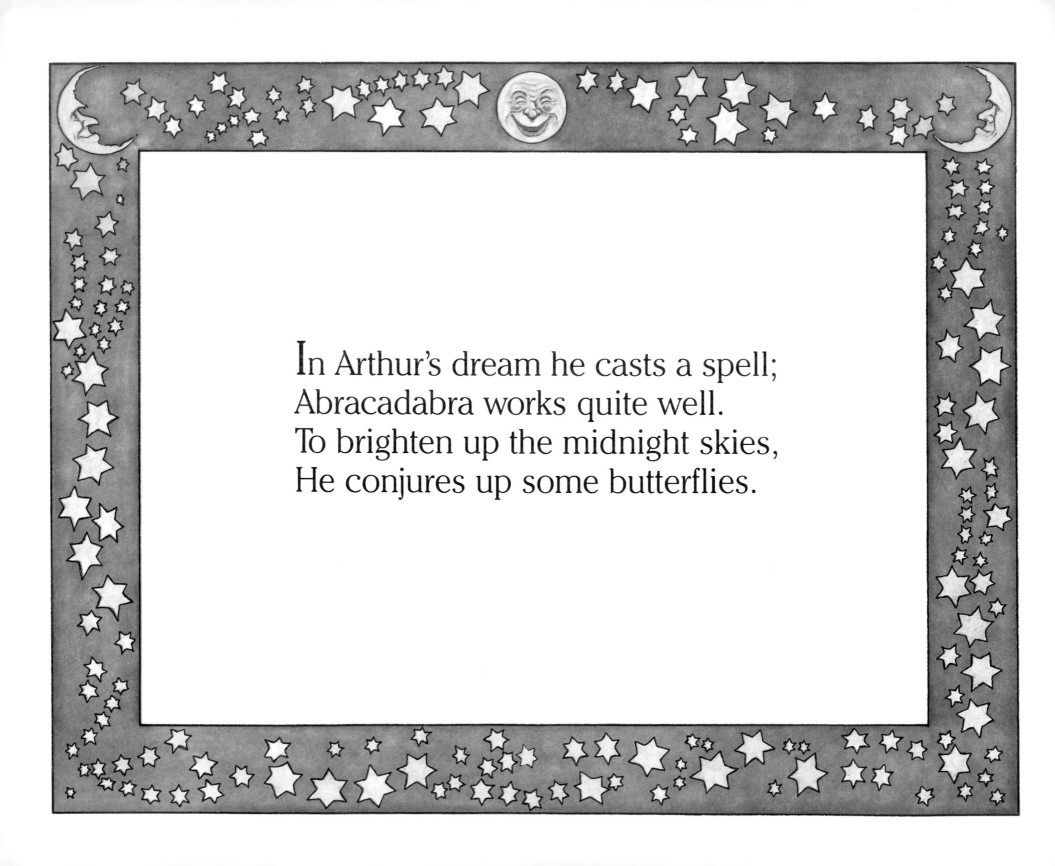

In Arthur's dream he casts a spell;
Abracadabra works quite well.
To brighten up the midnight skies,
He conjures up some butterflies.

The teddy bears have shared their dreams,
And these are but a few;
So now it's time to close your eyes,
And make your dream come true.